Mr. Gumpy's Outing

John Burningham

Henry Holt and Company · New York

Henry Holt and Company, LLC
Publishers since 1866
115 West 18th Street
New York, New York 10011

Henry Holt is a registered
trademark of Henry Holt and Company, LLC

First published in the United States by Henry Holt and Company
Published in Canada by Fitzhenry & Whiteside Ltd.,
195 Allstate Parkway, Markham, Ontario L3R 4T8.
Originally published in England by Jonathan Cape Ltd.

Library of Congress Catalog Card Number: 77-159507
ISBN 0-8050-0708-3
Designed by Jan Pienkowski
Printed in Mexico

25 24 23 22 21 20 19 18 17

This is Mr.Gumpy.

Mr. Gumpy owned a boat and his house was by a river.

One day Mr.Gumpy went out in his boat.

"May we come with you?" said the children.

"Yes," said Mr.Gumpy,
"if you don't squabble."

"Can I come along, Mr.Gumpy?"
said the rabbit.

"Yes, but don't hop about."

"I'd like a ride," said the cat.

"Very well," said Mr.Gumpy.
"But you're not to chase the rabbit."

"Will you take me with you?" said the dog.

"Yes," said Mr. Gumpy.
"But don't tease the cat."

"May I come, please, Mr. Gumpy?"
said the pig.

"Very well, but don't muck about."

"Have you a place for me?" said the sheep.

"Yes, but don't keep bleating."

"Can we come too?" said the chickens.

"Yes, but don't flap," said Mr. Gumpy.

"Can you make room for me?" said the calf.

"Yes, if you don't trample about."

"May I join you, Mr.Gumpy?" said the goat.

"Very well, but don't kick."

For a little while they all went along happily but then…

The goat kicked

The calf trampled

The chickens flapped

The sheep bleated

The pig mucked about

The dog teased the cat

The cat chased the rabbit

The rabbit hopped

The children squabbled

The boat tipped …

and into the water they fell.

Then Mr. Gumpy and the goat and the calf and the chickens and the sheep and the pig and the dog and the cat and the rabbit and the children all swam to the bank and climbed out to dry in the hot sun.

"We'll walk home across the fields," said Mr. Gumpy. "It's time for tea."

"Goodbye," said Mr. Gumpy.
"Come for a ride another day."